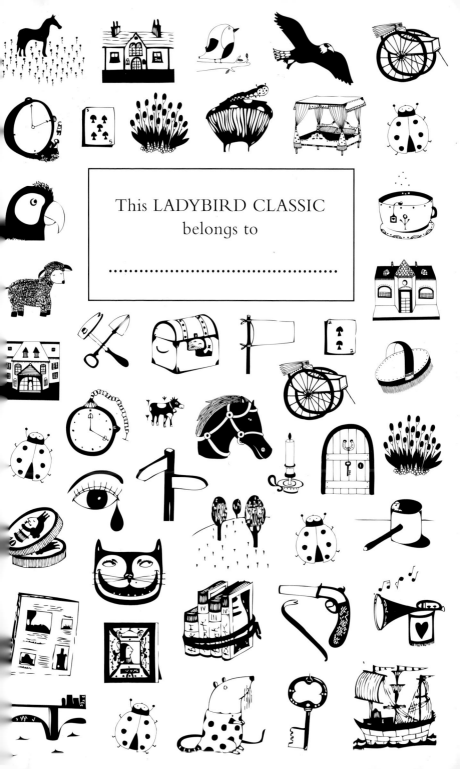

This LADYBIRD CLASSIC
belongs to

....

A History of the Author

Charles Dickens was born in 1812.
When he was 12 years old, his father,
a clerk, was imprisoned for debt, and
Charles was forced to work in a warehouse.
This experience affected him deeply, and
many stories and books he later wrote are
concerned with the hardships suffered
by the poor in Victorian England.

Chapter illustrations by Valeria Valenza

A catalogue record for this book is available from the British Library

Published by Ladybird Books Ltd
80 Strand London WC2R 0RL
A Penguin Company

001 – 10 9 8 7 6 5 4 3 2 1

© Ladybird Books Ltd MMXII

ISBN: 978-1-40931-221-5

Printed in China

LADYBIRD 🐞 CLASSICS

A Christmas Carol

by Charles Dickens

Retold by Joan Collins
Illustrated by Steve Horrocks

Contents

CHAPTER ONE
The Man Who Hated Christmas   7

CHAPTER TWO
Marley's Ghost   19

CHAPTER THREE
The Spirit of Christmas Past   27

CHAPTER FOUR
The Spirit of Christmas Present   37

CHAPTER FIVE
The Spirit of Christmas
Yet to Come   49

CHAPTER SIX
God Bless Us, Every One!   61

CHAPTER ONE

The Man Who Hated Christmas

THIS STORY BEGINS just after Queen
Victoria came to the throne. Jacob
Marley had been dead for seven years.
His business partner, Ebenezer Scrooge,
was the meanest man in London. He
would not even pay for a coat of paint
to remove Marley's name from the office
sign. It still read SCROOGE AND MARLEY.

It was a cold, foggy Christmas Eve.

Outside the office a small boy was singing
a carol:

'*God rest you merry gentlemen,*
Let nothing you dismay!'

Scrooge rushed out with a wooden ruler,
to take a crack at the boy's head. Just in
time, the boy scurried off.

Scrooge hated Christmas and
everything to do with it. He was a
tightfisted old miser, who never did a
kind deed nor gave a penny away. He
looked as if the cold had got right inside
him. His thin lips were blue. His eyebrows,
wiry hair and stubbly chin looked silver
with frost.

Coldest of all was Scrooge's heart.
It made his office feel chilly, even in
summer. At Christmas, it was freezing.
The fire was tiny, and Scrooge kept the
coal bucket by his desk. His clerk couldn't
fetch a piece of coal without asking.

The clerk's name was Bob Cratchit.

He sat on a high stool in the outer office, writing in a huge account book. Though he wore mittens, his fingers were so cold he could hardly hold is quill pen. He wore a long scarf he called his 'comforter' wrapped three times round his neck for warmth. His wife had knitted it, for Bob could not afford an overcoat. Scrooge only paid him fifteen shillings a week.

It was dark and foggy outside the office, but the people walking past were cheerful. The next day was Christmas, and the shops were blazing with lights and full of Christmas cheer. There were turkeys and geese, piles of oranges and apples, nuts, cakes and sweets – though not everyone had the money to buy them.

Suddenly Scrooge's office door opened and a cheery voice cried, 'Merry Christmas, Uncle!'

It was Scrooge's nephew, Fred. His face glowed with the cold, and his

eyes sparkled.

'Bah!' said Scrooge. 'Humbug! What reason have you to be merry? You're poor enough!'

His nephew laughed. 'What reason have you to be miserable? You're rich enough!'

'Merry Christmas!' growled Scrooge. 'Down with Christmas! If I had my way, every idiot that goes about saying "Merry Christmas" should be boiled with his own pudding and buried with a stake of holly through his heart!'

'You don't mean that, I'm sure, Uncle!' said Fred. 'Come and have Christmas dinner with us tomorrow, and let's be friends!'

But Scrooge refused.

'I'm going to wish you a merry Christmas in spite of your bad temper, Uncle,' said Fred. '*And* a Happy New Year!'

'Bah!' Scrooge snapped as his nephew left.

As Fred went out, he let in two gentlemen. They were collecting money for the poor, to give them a bit of comfort at Christmas time.

Scrooge refused to give the men anything at all. 'Are there no prisons?' he demanded. 'Are there no workhouses? I support those with my taxes. Let the poor go there!'

'Many can't go there,' said one of the men, 'and many would rather die.'

'Let them die, then!' said Scrooge. 'There are far too many poor people!'

The gentlemen went away, disappointed.

The fog got deeper and the afternoon darker. Soon it was time to shut the office. Bob Cratchit got ready to leave.

'I suppose you want the day off tomorrow,' Scrooge grumbled.

'If it's convenient, sir,' said Bob timidly.

'I shall have to pay you a whole day's

wages for no work!'

'It's only once a year,' said Bob.

'And that's once too often!' growled Scrooge, but he knew he had to let the clerk go. 'Just be sure to come earlier the following day, to make up for it!' he barked, as Bob left.

Bob ran off like a lad let out of school. He slid down a frozen hill twenty times, at the end of a line of boys. Then he hurried home to play Blind Man's Buff with his family.

Scrooge ate a lonely supper in a miserable inn, and read the financial papers.

CHAPTER TWO

Marley's Ghost

SCROOGE LIVED ALONE in rooms in a gloomy old house that had belonged to Jacob Marley. He was putting his key in the door when he noticed the big, old-fashioned knocker. There was something different about it tonight. It was... *Marley's face!*

Marley's face was a dismal shade of green. Ghostly spectacles were perched on its forehead, and its hair moved gently, as if a breeze were stirring it. As Scrooge stared, it turned back into a knocker again.

Scrooge was not frightened. He did not believe in ghosts. He entered the house, lit his candle and went up the wide staircase. He told himself firmly that Marley had been dead for seven years.

Upstairs everything was as usual. A saucepan of porridge was on the hob, by a small coal fire. Scrooge put on his slippers, dressing gown and nightcap, and sat down to eat his porridge. But first he made sure the door was locked.

There were pictures of Bible characters on the tiles around the fireplace – Cain and Abel, the Queen of Sheba, Abraham and Isaac. To Scrooge, they all bore the eerie look of Jacob Marley.

'Humbug!' said Scrooge.

Just then a bell high above the fireplace

began to swing to and fro. It had not been used for years, but now it began to ring loudly. Then came a clanking noise, deep in the house, as if someone were dragging a heavy chain up from the cellar.

'Humbug!' said Scrooge. 'I won't believe it!'

But the cellar door opened and the noise came up the stairs and into the room. The flame in the fire leapt up, as if to cry out in alarm, 'I know him! *Marley's ghost*!'

And there was Marley, wearing his usual waistcoat and tight trousers. A chain was wound round his waist, made of cash boxes, keys, padlocks, account books and metal purses. Scrooge could see right through Marley's body to the two buttons on the back of his coat.

'You don't believe in me, do you?' said the ghost.

'I don't,' said Scrooge. 'You could

be the result of an upset stomach. Perhaps you're a crumb of cheese, or an undigested bit of beef!'

The ghost took no notice of Scrooge's feeble joke. Instead, it gave a frightful cry and rattled its chain. 'I made this chain in life, link by link and yard by yard,' it said. 'You have one too, just as heavy as mine. But you have had seven years more, so yours is much longer.'

Scrooge looked down, but saw nothing.

'I only thought about money. I lost so many chances to do good,' sighed the ghost.

'But you were a good businessman, Jacob!'

'Business! Human beings were my business! I neglected them, and this is my punishment.'

'Why have you come to me?' asked Scrooge.

'To warn you, so that you can escape

my fate. You will be visited by three spirits. The first will come to you as the church clock strikes one.'

And then the ghost wrapped its chain round its arm and walked backwards towards the window, which opened wide. The ghost floated out into the night air.

Scrooge heard sad cries, and saw that the sky was full of figures like Marley. They were crying out and trying to reach the suffering human beings they had not helped while they were alive.

Suddenly Scrooge felt very tired. He crept into bed and fell asleep right away.

CHAPTER THREE

The Spirit of Christmas Past

SCROOGE WOKE WITH a start when
the church bell chimed midnight. Was a
spirit really going to appear to him at
one o'clock? He lay awake and listened;
at last the bell boomed out, 'ONE!'

The lights all flashed on in his room,
and the curtains on his four-poster bed
were drawn back. There stood a strange
small figure, with the smooth, tender face

of a child, but with long white hair like an old man's. It wore a white tunic and held a branch of holly in its hand. A bright, clear light shone from the top of its head. It wore a cap like a candle-snuffer, which it could use to put out this light.

'Who or what are you?' asked Scrooge.

'I am the Ghost of Christmas Past.'

'Long past?' asked Scrooge.

'No,' replied the spirit. 'Your past.'

'What brings you here?'

'To remind you,' said the spirit. 'To help you. Get up and come with me!'

Scrooge got out of bed in his nightclothes and took the spirit's hand.

They were suddenly in a small town in the country. Boys were riding along the road, some on ponies, some in farmers' carts, calling to one another happily. They were going home for the Christmas holidays. Scrooge knew who they were – his old school friends.

He began to cry. He remembered how he had been left behind that Christmas, in a cold, gloomy schoolroom, forgotten by everyone. He saw himself as a boy, reading quietly. Behind him, outside the window, the people in the book came to life.

'There's Robinson Crusoe with his parrot, and Man Friday running along the beach!' Scrooge called out excitedly. But the pictures faded. He dried his eyes on his sleeve. 'I wish...' he said.

'What?' asked the ghost.

'There was a boy singing carols outside my office tonight,' said Scrooge. 'I wish I'd given him something.'

The spirit waved its hand. 'Let's look at another Christmas,' it said.

It was the same schoolroom. The boy was older, alone again. Suddenly the door opened and a little girl rushed in and hugged him. It was his sister. She'd been

sent to bring him home for Christmas.

'She was never strong. She died young,' said Scrooge.

'And left one child, I believe,' said the spirit. 'Your nephew.'

'Yes,' said Scrooge thoughtfully.

Then they left the school behind, and found themselves in a huge city. It was Christmas Eve, and the streets were lit up. They stopped at a warehouse door.

'Do you know it?' asked the spirit.

'Know it? I was apprenticed here!' said Scrooge excitedly.

There was a jolly party in full swing. Old Fezziwig, Scrooge's employer, was celebrating with his family and workers. There was a splendid supper: cold meats, mince pies, cake and beer. Best of all, there was a fiddler, who played lively music for country dancing!

Mr and Mrs Fezziwig were the top couple in 'Sir Roger de Coverley'. Old

Fezziwig seemed to be everywhere at once, and Mrs Fezziwig kept up with him! Scrooge was delighted. He enjoyed it all as much as he had all those years ago. At the end, he looked up at the spirit.

'Is anything the matter?' asked the spirit.

'No,' said Scrooge. 'I just wish I could say a word to my clerk, that's all.'

The next picture was not so cheerful. Scrooge was older and looked meaner. He was talking to his sweetheart. She was saying that he cared more about money than about her, and she gave him back his engagement ring. Next, he saw his sweetheart happily married to someone else, while he sat alone in his office.

'Take me away!' he cried out. He struggled with the spirit, trying to press the cap down on the Light of Memory

that shone from its head. Suddenly he
was in his own bedroom. He fell on his
bed, and sank into a deep sleep.

CHAPTER FOUR

The Spirit of Christmas Present

SCROOGE WOKE AGAIN with
a jump, just as the clock was striking.
A blaze of light shone in the next room.
He heard a voice calling him.

Scrooge put on his slippers and shuffled
to the door. He was astonished to see that
the room was decorated with holly, ivy
and mistletoe, and there was a huge fire
in the grate. Heaped up on the floor, to

make a kind of throne, were roast turkeys, geese, joints of beef, sausages, mince pies, Christmas puddings and pyramids of fruit. On top of the heap sat a jolly giant, holding a torch shaped like a Horn of Plenty.

'Come in, man, and get to know me!' said the giant. 'I am the Ghost of Christmas Present!'

The spirit was dressed in a deep green robe edged with white fur, and wore a holly wreath on his brown curly hair.

'I know you have come to do me good,' said Scrooge humbly. 'Please take me with you and show me your message.'

The spirit took him out into the streets, where people were doing their last-minute Christmas shopping. Church bells rang out. Poor people, who could not afford the fuel to cook at home, were carrying their dinners to the bakers' shops. The spirit sprinkled a few drops from his torch,

in blessing, on the poor folks' dinners.

They came to a very small house. It belonged to Bob Cratchit, Scrooge's clerk. The spirit gave this house a special blessing.

The Cratchits were all dressed up in honour of Christmas. Mrs Cratchit and her daughters had shabby dresses, but they had decked them out with bright ribbons. Young Peter was sticking a fork into a bubbling saucepan of potatoes, while one of the girls laid the table.

'Here come Father and Tiny Tim!' cried the children, as Bob, with Tiny Tim on his shoulder, came through the door. Tiny Tim carried a crutch and had an iron frame on his leg.

Just then two young Cratchits came charging in from the baker's, bringing the goose on a tray! Mrs Cratchit heated up the gravy. Peter mashed the potatoes. The girls dished up the apple sauce and put

out the warm plates. Everyone sat round the table, and Bob said grace. Then Mrs Cratchit plunged her carving knife into the breast, and the smell of sage and onion stuffing gushed out.

They all said there never was such a tender, tasty goose. And there was enough for everyone!

Next it was the turn of the Christmas pudding, which had been boiling away in the kitchen copper. Mrs Cratchit carried it in, blazing with brandy and with a sprig of holly on top. No one even dared to hint that it was rather a small pudding for such a big family!

At last they all sat round the fire, eating roast chestnuts and drinking Christmas toasts. 'I wish a Merry Christmas to us all, my dear!' said Bob. 'God bless us!'

'God bless us, every one!' added Tiny Tim. He sat beside his father, who held his thin little hand.

'Spirit,' whispered Scrooge, 'tell me if Tiny Tim will live.'

'I see an empty chair,' said the spirit, 'and beside it a little crutch. If these shadows do not change, Tiny Tim will not see another Christmas. But why should you care? Let him die. There are too many poor people.'

Hearing his own words, Scrooge was silent with shame.

Then the spirit showed Scrooge what Christmas meant to people in lonely, faraway places. To miners below the earth. To men in lighthouses, surrounded by sea and storm. To sailors on board ship in the dark night, singing carols as they worked.

Suddenly Scrooge heard a jolly laugh. It was Fred, his nephew. He was having a Christmas party, and they were playing a guessing game. Fred had to think of something, and could only answer 'yes' or 'no' to questions about it.

Yes, he was thinking of an animal
– a savage, disagreeable animal. Yes,
it lived in London. No, it wasn't in
a zoo. No, it wasn't a horse… or a
donkey… or a tiger… or a cat…
or a bear. Fred laughed so much he
almost fell off the sofa.

At last his plump sister-in-law squealed
out, 'I know who it is! It's your Uncle
Scroo-oo-ge!'

And so it was! They all drank a toast to
Uncle Scrooge, who would have answered
them, but the spirit took him away again.

Gradually, the spirit grew smaller and
smaller. His brown hair turned to grey.

'Is your life so short?' asked Scrooge.

'Yes. It ends at midnight.'

Then Scrooge noticed something hiding
in the folds of the spirit's robe. There were
two children sheltering there, a boy and a
girl, very thin, half-starved and ragged.

'These are the children of the world

who have no parents, and no one to make a Christmas for them,' said the spirit sadly.

'Have they nowhere to go?' asked Scrooge.

'Are there no prisons?' said the spirit, turning on him with his own words. 'Are there no workhouses?'

The clock struck twelve.

Scrooge looked about for the spirit, but it was gone. Instead, he saw a solemn figure, clad in a dark hood and cloak, gliding like a mist over the ground towards him. It was the last of the spirits.

CHAPTER FIVE

The Spirit of Christmas Yet to Come

THE SPIRIT DID not speak. All Scrooge could see of it in the gloom was one outstretched hand, pointing from its black garments. Scrooge was filled with fear.

'Are you the Spirit of the Future?' he asked, trembling. 'Are you going to show me things that are going to happen in years to come?'

The spirit seemed to bend its head.

'Will you not speak to me?' begged Scrooge.

The spirit merely pointed straight ahead.

They were in the City. Businessmen were standing in groups, chinking the coins in their pockets. Scrooge and the spirit stopped near enough to hear what some of them were saying.

'I don't know much about it,' said one fat merchant. 'I only know he's dead.'

'Who's he left all his money to?' asked another, taking snuff out of a large snuffbox.

'*I* don't know,' said a red-faced banker with a wart on his nose. 'He hasn't left it to *me*!' They all laughed.

'I wonder who'll go to his funeral,' said the fat man. 'He hadn't any friends.'

Scrooge wondered who they were talking about. He looked about for himself, but he was not in his usual place of business.

Next the spirit took Scrooge to a dreadful slum in the poorest part of London. Under a low roof there stood a shabby old secondhand shop, full of rubbish. A rag-and-bone man crouched by an evil-smelling stove, waiting for customers.

Two men and a woman came in out of the murky night, carrying bundles. They had some bedding, clothes and old curtains to sell.

'Where'd you get these, then?' croaked the rag-and-bone merchant, picking them over.

'The old chap we took them from won't want them again,' chuckled the woman.

'If he hadn't been such a wicked old screw, he might have had someone to look after him when he was dying,' said one of the men, throwing down a pair of cufflinks. 'It serves him right.'

Scrooge watched as a few coins changed hands.

'Spirit,' he said, 'doesn't anyone feel anything about this man's death?'

The ghost spread its dark robe out like a wing and then drew it back to show a room where a mother sat with her young children. Her husband came in, looking ill and worried. Yet there was a look of joy in his face, too.

'We have more time to pay our debt,' he said.

'Has the old man relented, then?' asked his wife eagerly.

'No,' said her husband. 'He is dead.'

The wife's face brightened. The only feeling anyone had for the old man's death was relief.

Scrooge begged the spirit to show him some kinder feeling connected with a death. In reply, the spirit took him to

Bob Cratchit's house.

The little Cratchits were quiet. Their mother was sewing. 'Your father is late tonight,' she said.

'I think he walks slower in the evening than he did with Tiny Tim on his shoulder,' said Peter.

'Your father loved Tiny Tim, and he was so light to carry,' said their mother.

Just then Bob came in, and his family hurried to get his tea. He had been to the cemetery.

'It's a lovely place,' said Bob. 'I promised Tiny Tim we'd go there every Sunday. We must never forget Tiny Tim. And we must never quarrel with one another, for he was so patient and good.'

They all hugged one another, and promised.

Scrooge said anxiously to the spirit, 'Show me myself as I shall be in years to come!'

The spirit took him to his office, but another man sat at his desk. Scrooge began to feel a sense of dread.

Still pointing, the tall black figure took Scrooge to an iron gate that led to a neglected churchyard, where the grass and the nettles had grown high. The spirit stood among the graves and, with its long finger, pointed to one.

'Before I look at that grave,' said Scrooge, 'tell me, Spirit, are these things that *will* happen, or are they things that *may* happen?'

The spirit just continued to point at the grave without speaking. Scrooge crept towards it and, trembling, read: EBENEZER SCROOGE.

'No, no!' cried Scrooge, clutching the spirit's robe. 'I am not that man! I will not be that man! Isn't there any hope for me? Can I change what you have shown me?'

Ebenezer
Scrooge

The spirit's hand trembled.

'I promise to keep Christmas in my heart, all the year round! I promise to remember the lessons the spirits have taught me – Christmas Past, Christmas Present and Christmas Future! Please tell me I can change the writing on this stone!'

As he begged the spirit, he saw an alteration in its hood and dress. It shrank, collapsed and changed – into a bedpost.

Chapter Six

God Bless Us, Every One!

IT WAS SCROOGE'S own bedpost, and his own room! And it was his own time ahead to make up for the past.

He scrambled out of bed and clutched the bed curtains. They had not been torn down and sold! He put on his clothes, inside out, upside down, any way, laughing and crying at the same time.

'A Merry Christmas, everybody!' he

shouted. 'A Happy New Year to all
the world!'

He heard the church bells ringing out.
Clash, clash, hammer, ding, dong! The fog
had cleared, and there was golden sunlight
and fresh morning air. Scrooge flung open
the window.

'What day is it?' he called to a boy in
the street.

'What day? Why, Christmas Day!'

Scrooge had not lost any time after
all! The spirits had shown him all their
wonders in one night, and it was still
Christmas morning.

'Do you know the butcher's in the
next street?' Scrooge called down to
the boy.

'Of course!' replied the boy.

'Go and tell the butcher I want the
biggest turkey in the shop – the Prize
Turkey. Bring the man back with you so
that I can tell him where to take it, and

I'll give you half a crown!'

The boy ran off down the street, and came back with the splendid turkey.

'I'll send it to Bob Cratchit,' chuckled Scrooge. 'He won't know where it came from. It's twice the size of Tiny Tim!'

After he had sent the man off with the turkey, he had a good look at the door knocker. 'What an honest expression it has! It's a wonderful knocker!' he said, stepping back inside.

Scrooge shaved, dressed up in his best suit and went out. He smiled at all the people he met and wished them a Merry Christmas, and they returned the greeting. Then he spotted one of the gentlemen who had been collecting for the poor. He went up and whispered something in his ear. The gentlemen looked amazed and delighted.

'A great many back payments are included in that!' said Scrooge.

Next he marched boldly up to his nephew's front door and rang the bell.

'It's your Uncle Scrooge,' he said. 'I have come to have dinner. Will you let me in, Fred?'

Of course he would! Fred nearly shook Scrooge's hand off. They had the most wonderful dinner party, and Scrooge joined in it all – games, dancing, and carol singing.

Next morning Scrooge was up early. He wanted to catch Bob Cratchit coming late to the office. Sure enough, poor Bob tried to sneak in unnoticed, nearly twenty minutes after his usual time. He got rid of his hat and comforter and jumped on his stool, writing away as if his life depended on it.

Scrooge glowered at him, pretending to be his old horrible self. 'What do you mean by coming in at this time of day?' he snapped.

'I'm very sorry,' said Bob meekly. 'It's only once a year.'

'I'm not going to stand this sort of thing any longer,' said Scrooge, giving Bob a dig in the waistcoat, 'and therefore' – giving him another dig, which pushed him right back into the outer office – 'therefore – I am about to raise your wages!'

Bob thought Scrooge had gone mad! He looked about for the long wooden ruler, in case he needed to defend himself.

'A Merry Christmas, Bob,' said Scrooge. 'A Merrier Christmas than I have given you for many a year, my poor fellow! Make up the fire – let's have a real blaze – and fetch another bucket of coal! I'll look after your family and help Tiny Tim – and we'll brew up a hot toddy this afternoon to celebrate!'

Scrooge was better than his word. He did all that he said and more, and to Tiny Tim (who did *not* die) he was

a second father.

Scrooge became as good a friend, as good a master and as good a man as the good old City of London knew, or any city in the good old world!

He saw no more spirits. But it was said of him that he knew how to keep Christmas as well as any man alive.

May that be true of all of us. And, as Tiny Tim once said, 'God Bless Us, Every One!'

Collect more fantastic

LADYBIRD  CLASSICS

Alice in Wonderland

9781409311232

Oliver Twist

9781409311256

Treasure Island

9781409311287

BLACK BEAUTY

9781409311249

GULLIVER'S Travels

9781409311270

The Secret Garden

9781409311263

A Christmas Carol

9781409312215

Peter Pan

9781409312222